THE LEAKY UMBRELLA

THE LEAKY UMBRELLA

by Demi

PRENTICE-HALL, INC.
ENGLEWOOD CLIFFS, NEW JERSEY

Printed in the United States of America J

Prentice-Hall International, Inc., London
Prentice-Hall of Australia, Pty. Ltd., North Sydney
Prentice-Hall of Canada, Ltd., Toronto
Prentice-Hall of India Private Ltd., New Delhi
Prentice-Hall of Japan, Inc., Tokyo
Prentice-Hall of Southeast Asia Pte. Ltd., Singapore
Whitehall Books Limited, Wellington, New Zealand

1 2 3 4 5 6 7 8 9 10

DESIGNED BY ERNIE HAIM

Once upon a time
                in Japan
there was a man named Wako
who liked to daydream.

One day
        when he
went outside for a walk
it started to rain.

"I need
    an umbrella,"
Wako thought.

He stopped
        at a big house
to borrow one.

There was
         an umbrella
hanging on the wall,

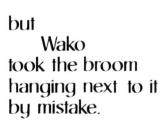

but
      Wako
took the broom
hanging next to it
by mistake.

Wako said,
"Thank you,"
bowed low and walked outside again.

He held
   the broom up
over his head like an umbrella.

But who
do you think he saw?

There
was Oho,
his best friend,
out in the rain
and without an umbrella.

Oho said,
        "I'm glad I met you!
Please let me in under your umbrella."
"Certainly," said Wako, "
and keep close to me
or else you will get wet."

People
were amazed
to see a broom bobbing
up and down in the air.

But
    Oho and Wako
were so busy talking
they didn't notice anything at all.

When
they were
almost home
Oho suddenly said,
"Look how wet we're getting
even though we have an umbrella!"

"Yes, replied Wako,

"This umbrella leaks."

MORAL: Heaven weeps over fools.